This book belongs to

CARIBBEAN SEA

Characters (in order of appearance)
Narrator — DIEDRICH BADER
Captain Jack Sparrow — JOHNNY DEPP
Leech — SAN SHELLA
Joshamee Gibbs — KEVIN R. MCNALLY
Bootstrap Bill Turner — STELLAN SKARSGÅRD
Lord Cutler Beckett — TOM HOLLANDER
Will Turner — ORLANDO BLOOM
Elizabeth Swann — KEIRA KNIGHTLEY
Tia Dalma — NAOMIE HARRIS
Davy Jones — BILL NIGHY
Maccus — DERMOT KEANEY
James Norrington — JACK DAVENPORT

Read-along Story Produced by RANDY THORNTON
and TED KRYCZKO
Co-produced and Engineered by JEFF SHERIDAN
and DAN MONTES
Adapted by BARBARA BAZULDUA, RANDY THORNTON
and TED KRYCZKO
Creative Direction by STEVE GERDES
Design by STEVE STERLING
℗ WALT DISNEY RECORDS
Motion Picture Artwork, Photos, TM & Copyright
© 2006 Disney Enterprises, Inc.

Printed in China
First Edition
10 9 8 7 6 5 4 3 2 1
Library of Congress Catalog Card Number: 2006901713
ISBN 1-4231-0368-8
Visit DISNEYPIRATES.COM

Based on the screenplay written by Ted Elliott & Terry Rossio
Based on characters created by Ted Elliott & Terry Rossio
and Stuart Beattie and Jay Wolpert
Based on Walt Disney's Pirates of the Caribbean
Produced by Jerry Bruckheimer
Directed by Gore Verbinski

New York

High on the walls of a Turkish prison overlooking the sea, Captain Jack Sparrow hid in a wooden coffin, waiting for the guards to toss it into the ocean. As it hit the waves, Jack scrambled out. In his hand, he clutched a drawing of a key.

Back onboard his ship, the *Black Pearl*, Jack showed the drawing to his crew. "Gentlemen, what do keys do?"

"Keys unlock things?"

"And whatever this key unlocks, inside there's something valuable. So we're setting out to find whatever this key unlocks."

"No! If we don't have the key, we can't open whatever it is we don't have that it unlocks. So what purpose would be served in finding whatever need be unlocked, which we don't have, without first having found the key what unlocks it?"

So they set off to find the key. But Jack's Compass wasn't working properly, and he didn't know which way to sail.

That night as Jack paced the deck, a pale figure stepped from the shadows. It was Bootstrap Bill with a message. "Time's run out, Jack. He sent me. Davy Jones. You made a deal with him too, Jack. He raised the *Pearl* from the depths for you. Thirteen years you've been a captain."

"Technically—"

"Jack, you won't be able to talk yourself out of this. The terms what apply to me, apply to you as well. One soul, bound to crew a hundred years upon a ship …"

"Yes, but the *Flying Dutchman* already has a captain, so there's really no—"

"Then it's The Locker for you! Jones's terrible leviathan will find you, and will drag the *Pearl* back to the depths and you along with it!"

As Bootstrap spoke, a Black Spot appeared on Jack's hand. Terrified, he shouted at his crew. "On deck, all hands! Run, keep running!"

"Do we have a heading?"

"Run! Land!"

"Which port?"

"Didn't say port, I said land! Any land!"

Meanwhile, in Port Royal, Elizabeth Swann and Will Turner had their own troubles. Lord Cutler Beckett, head of the East India Trading Company, had arrested them for piracy. Beckett addressed his prisoner. "By your efforts, Jack Sparrow was set free. I would like you to go to him and recover a certain property in his possession."

"Recover? At the point of a sword?"

"Bargain. You will offer what amounts to a full pardon. Jack will be free, a privateer in the employ of England. Jack must find his place in the New World or perish. Not unlike you, Mr. Turner. You and your fiancée face the hangman's noose."

"So you get both Jack and the *Black Pearl*."

"A ship? Hardly. The item in question's considerably smaller and far more valuable. Something Sparrow keeps on his person at all times—a compass. Bring back that Compass or there's no deal."

Will accepted the deal. He left to tell Elizabeth, who was still being held in a prison cell. Elizabeth was worried. "Jack's Compass. What does Beckett want with that?"

"Does it matter?"

"I have faith in you. Both of you." But when Will left, Elizabeth began making her own plans.

Will searched the seas for days. At last, he spied the *Black Pearl* stranded on the beach of a deserted island. A deathly silence hung over the island. Will's shouts echoed strangely as he thrashed through the deep jungle. "Jack! Jack Sparrow!"

Meanwhile in Port Royal, Elizabeth escaped her prison cell, sneaked into Beckett's offices, and held him at gunpoint. "I'm here to negotiate."

"I'm listening intently."

"These Letters of Marque, they are signed by the King?"

"You're making great efforts to ensure Jack Sparrow's freedom."

"These aren't going to Jack."

"Oh, really? To ensure Mr. Turner's freedom, then? I'll still want that Compass."

Disguising herself as a sailor, she stowed away on a ship to go in search of Will.

As Will crashed through the jungle, cannibals surrounded him. Numbing him with poison darts, they carried him to their village. There on a throne of bones and skulls sat Jack Sparrow. "Jack! It's me, Will Turner. Tell them to let me down!"

To Will's confusion and anger, Jack ignored him. But as the cannibals dragged Will away, Jack leaned towards him slightly. "Save me!"

Will was horrified when he realized the truth. Jack was a captive, too!

High above a gorge hung two cages made of human bones and jammed full of Jack's pirate crew. The cannibals shoved Will inside a cage with Jack's first mate, Gibbs.

"The Pelegostos made Jack their chief. But he only remains chief as long as he acts like a chief. The Pelegostos believe that Jack is a god in human form and they intend to do him the honor of releasing him from his fleshy prison. They'll roast him and eat him. The feast is about to begin. Jack's life will end when the drums stop."

Will knew he had to do something. He ordered the pirates to swing the cages toward the canyon walls where thick vines grew. Rocking back and forth, the pirates grasped the vines. "Come on, men!"

"Put your legs through! Start to climb!"

But as they reached the top of the gorge, a cannibal guard saw them. He raced for the village shouting the alarm.

Screaming in anger, the cannibals raced after the escaping pirates, leaving Jack alone. Taking his final chance to escape, Jack jerked himself free and sped toward the beach where the *Black Pearl* waited. He reached it just as Will and the rest of his crew raced up. Dodging hordes of screeching cannibals, the men leapt onboard and cast off. Gibbs greeted his captain. "Let's put some distance between us and this island and head out to open sea."

"Yes to the first, yes to the second, but only in so far as we keep to the shallows as much as possible!"

Safe for a time, Will asked Jack for his Compass. "Jack, Elizabeth is in danger. I need that Compass of yours, Jack. I must trade it for her freedom."

Finally, Jack made Will a deal. "I shall trade you the Compass if you will help me … to find this." He showed him the drawing of an unusual key. When Will agreed, Jack told him there was only one person who could tell them where it was—the mysterious Tia Dalma.

Later that night, they rowed up a dark swampy river to Tia Dalma's rambling shack. She was waiting for them as if she had known they would come.

Tia Dalma nodded knowingly when Jack showed her the drawing of the key. "Your key go to a chest. And it is what lay inside the chest you seek, don't it? You know of … Davy Jones, yes?"

"What exactly did he put into the chest?"

"Him heart. Him carve out him heart. Lock it away in a chest, and hide the chest from the world. The key? He keep with him at all times."

To get it, Will would have to sneak onboard the *Flying Dutchman* ship and take the key from Jones. Tia Dalma told them where to seek the ghostly ship, and she gave Jack a jar of dirt. "Davy Jones cannot step on land but once every ten years. Land is where you are safe, Jack Sparrow, and so you will carry land with you."

V ⚙ ⚓

As Jack and Will searched for the *Flying Dutchman*, they saw a shipwreck on a rocky shore. Jack's blood ran cold. This was the work of Davy Jones. As Will prepared to board the ship, Jack gave him some advice. "If you do happen to get captured, just say Jack Sparrow sent you to settle his debt. Might save your life."

On the ship deck, Will saw faceless dead men scattered everywhere. Suddenly, the wind began to howl and the ghostly *Flying Dutchman* rose from the churning sea. Moments later, Davy Jones stood before Will. "What is your purpose here?"

"Jack Sparrow … sent me to settle his debt."

Davy Jones was furious!

Onboard the *Black Pearl*, Jack watched and waited.

Suddenly he heard Davy Jones's angry voice behind him. "You have a debt to pay."

"You have my payment: one soul to serve on your ship. He's already over there."

"One soul is not equal to another."

"Just how many souls do you think my soul is worth?"

Desperate to escape his dreaded fate, Jack bargained with Jones. He would bring him one hundred souls in three days in exchange for his own freedom. Jones agreed.

"I keep the boy. A good faith payment. That leaves you only ninety-nine more to go."

It seemed that Will would be doomed forever.

V · ⚙ · ⛵

Jack and his crew sailed to Tortuga to find souls for Davy Jones. There, they met Jack's old enemy, James Norrington. Desperate and half-crazed, Norrington signed on. To Jack's amazement, so did someone else. Elizabeth Swann. She wanted Jack's help finding Will.

Jack gave Elizabeth his Compass. "Poor Will has been press-ganged into Davy Jones's crew."

"All I want is to find Will."

"Well, there is a chest of unknown size and origin. And whoever possesses that chest, possesses the leverage to command Jones to do whatever it is he or she wants. With this. This Compass does not point north. It points to the thing you want most in this world. And what you want most in this world is to find the chest of Davy Jones, is it not?"

"To save Will."

"By finding the chest of Davy Jones."

In Elizabeth's hands, the Compass worked! Steadily the needle swung around until it pointed to *Isla Cruces* … the Isle of Crosses.

V   ✴   ⛴

Aboard the *Flying Dutchman*, Will waited and watched for his
chance to get the key. At last, one night, while Jones slept, Will crept
into his quarters and carefully removed the key from the chain around
his neck. Then he hurried to the longboat where his father waited.
"Now get yourself to land, and stay there. It was always in my blood
to die at sea, but it was not a fate I ever wanted for you."

"I'll find a way to sever Jones's hold on you and not rest until this
blade pierces his heart." With that, Will rowed away into the night.

V ⚙ ⛵

Many long, wet, cold hours later, a passing trading ship rescued Will
from the longboat. Will begged the ship's captain to sail away as fast
as he could. But it was too late. The *Flying Dutchman* was on the horizon.
Will grew pale. "I've doomed us all."

With a sickening jolt, the ship lurched to a stop. The sea boiled
with foam as a huge, slimy tentacle rose from the waves. Will
watched, powerless, as it snatched the captain, threw him into the air,
and broke him like a twig. It was the Kraken, sent by Jones to destroy
Will and whoever helped him.

Nothing and no one could stop it. Its huge tentacles swept screaming
sailors into the sea, smashed the longboats, and snapped the mast in
two. Will fell overboard. As he sank beneath the waves, he saw the
Kraken pull the ship down. In an instant, all that was left was a trail
of shattered wood and broken bodies.

V ⚙ ⛵

The shadow of the *Flying Dutchman* drifted above Will as he surfaced. He snatched at its hull and hauled himself up, clinging to a small crack in the wood. Above him, he heard one of the crew tell Davy Jones some disturbing news. "The boy's not here. He must have been claimed by the sea."

"I am the sea. The chest is no longer safe. Chart a course to *Isla Cruces*. Get me there first or there'll be the devil to pay!"

Wet, and shaking with cold, Will hung on. He was still alive. And he would reach *Isla Cruces* with Davy Jones.

At last, Jack and his crew reached *Isla Cruces* and rowed ashore. Elizabeth led Jack and Norrington toward an ancient abandoned church. Then she stopped with a confused look. The compass needle suddenly began to spin. "This doesn't work. And it certainly doesn't show you what you want most!"

"Yes it does. You're sitting on it."

"Beg pardon?"

Jack pushed her aside as he and Norrington began to dig. They quickly uncovered a large chest. Inside it was a small chest of solid iron. And from inside that they heard the rhythm of a muffled heartbeat.

No one saw the *Flying Dutchman* approach. As the cursed crew prepared to go ashore, Will swam to the beach. In no time, he found Jack, Elizabeth, and Norrington staring at the iron chest before them.

"It's real."

"You actually were telling the truth."

"I do that quite a lot. Yet people are always surprised."

"With good reason!" It was Will! He pushed his way through and made for the chest. "I'm going to kill Jones."

"I can't let you do that William. 'Cause if Jones is dead, who's to call his terrible beastie off the hunt, hey?" Only Davy Jones could control the Kraken. If Jones died, the monster would never stop. Jack's plan was to use the chest to make Jones call his monster off forever. Then Norrington stepped between them. He wanted to take the chest to Lord Cutler Beckett. Each man needed the chest for different reasons. They drew their swords, charged each other, and began to battle for the key.

As Jack and the others fought, Jones's crew rose from the sea. Jack snatched the key from Will and opened the chest. He grabbed the heart, dashed to the beach, and stuffed it into his jar of dirt. But Jones's crew surrounded them. There was no escape.

Suddenly, Norrington grabbed the chest and ran, drawing the fiends away. "Into the boat. Don't wait for me." As the ghoulish crew closed in, Norrington dropped the chest. "Here you go." In a flash, the crew and the chest disappeared.

As the *Black Pearl* sped away, the *Flying Dutchman* shot up from the depths beside it and opened fire. Jack dropped his jar and it shattered at his feet. The heart was gone!

Groaning, the *Black Pearl* shuddered to a stop. In the deathly silence, the Kraken rose from the sea. Will shouted orders to the terrified crew. "To arms! Run out the cannons and hold for my signal! Fire!"

Blasted by the cannons, the Kraken drew back, but Will knew it would attack again.

"We have to get off the ship." But the Kraken had destroyed all the longboats, except one. And Jack Sparrow was in it, rowing toward land.

Will and the crew loaded the cargo net with barrels of gunpowder and swung it out over the rail. Then Will gave Elizabeth a rifle. "Whatever you do, don't miss!" He leapt on top and called out to the Kraken. "Come on! Come and get it, I'm over here!"

With a roar, the Kraken shot up, tangling its tentacles on the cargo net.

As Elizabeth took aim, the ship lurched and she fell. Then she saw Jack. His Compass had pointed him back to the *Black Pearl* ... and her. Jack grabbed the rifle and fired as Will leapt away. The gunpowder exploded, ripping the Kraken's tentacles apart and setting them on fire. Again, the Kraken fell back, but Jack knew it would return.

"Abandon ship. Into the longboat."

Will and the crew rushed for the longboat, but Elizabeth turned to Jack. "You came back. I always knew you were a good man." And then she kissed him … a long kiss that lasted as she pushed him backwards. Jack heard a loud click and opened his eyes. Elizabeth had chained him to the mast. "It's after you, not the ship … it's not us. This is the only way, don't you see? I'm not sorry."

Jack smiled at Elizabeth. "Pirate."

Elizabeth raced to the longboat and climbed in with Will and the others.

Will looked around. "Where's Jack?"

"He elected to stay behind to give us a chance. Go!"

From a distance, Will, Elizabeth, and the crew watched the Kraken pull the *Black Pearl* beneath the waves. Jack Sparrow had gone down with his ship.

Onboard the *Flying Dutchman*, Davy Jones's men set his chest down before him. He smiled as he began to open it. "Jack Sparrow, our debt is settled." Seconds later, a terrible roar of anger rang out. His heart was gone.

Far away in Port Royal, Norrington was brought before Lord Cutler Beckett. He placed the pardon documents, promised to Will and Elizabeth, before him. "I took the liberty of filling in my name."

"If you intend to claim these, then you must have something to trade. Do you have the Compass?"

"Better." He placed a burlap sack on Beckett's desk. "The heart of Davy Jones."

The crafty Beckett smiled.

V ☸ ⚓

Days later, Will, Elizabeth, and Gibbs sat with Tia Dalma in her shack, remembering Jack. She studied them closely. "Will you sail to the ends of the earth and beyond to fetch back witty Jack?"

They stared at her as if she was crazy. Then as one person, they shouted, "Aye!"

Tia Dalma was pleased. "All right. But if you're goin' brave the weird and haunted shoals at world's end, then you will need a captain who knows those waters."

At the top of her stairs the door opened and Captain Barbossa walked into the room.